No Babysitters Allowed

No Babysit

Amber Stewart

ters Allowed

illustrated by Laura Rankin

BLOOMSBURY CHILDREN'S BOOKS

Published by Bloomsbury U.S.A. Children's Books
175 Fifth Avenue, New York, New York 10010

Library of Congress Cataloging-in-Publication Data
Stewart, Amber.
No babysitters allowed / by Amber Stewart ; illustrations by Laura Rankin. — 1st U.S. ed.
p.   cm.
Summary: Hopscotch is a very brave young rabbit until
his parents go out and leave him with a babysitter.
ISBN-13: 978-1-59990-154-1 · ISBN-10: 1-59990-154-4 (hardcover)
ISBN-13: 978-1-59990-313-2 · ISBN-10: 1-59990-313-X (reinforced)
[1. Fear—Fiction. 2. Babysitting—Fiction. 3. Rabbits—Fiction.]
I. Rankin, Laura, ill. II. Title.
PZ7.S84868No 2008   [E]—dc22   2008002406

Art created with acrylics and pen and ink on Arches 140-lb cold press watercolor paper
Typeset in Cheltenham Light
Book design by Donna Mark

First U.S. Edition 2008
Printed in China
2 4 6 8 10 9 7 5 3 1 (hardcover)
2 4 6 8 10 9 7 5 3 1 (reinforced)

For my mum
—A. S.

In loving memory of my mother,
Mary Rankin
—L. R.

Hopscotch was a brave boy.

He was so brave he could take a spider that came visiting
back out to the garden when Mommy was scared,

and when he fell off his tricycle and had to have a
Band-Aid on his leg, he didn't cry at all.

There were many things that Hopscotch could do
very, very bravely.

But when Hopscotch realized that tonight was a
Mrs.-Honeybunch-the-babysitter night,

he didn't feel brave at all.

"Sweetheart," Mommy said,
"don't you like Mrs. Honeybunch?"
"No," said Hopscotch. "Rabbity and
I do not like Mrs. Honeybunch."

But really, Hopscotch didn't like bedtime without
Mommy and Daddy. It made him feel all worried inside,
and that made his tummy hurt.

"I have a tummy ache, Mommy," Hopscotch said hopefully. "You can't go out when my tummy is worried."

"Mrs. Honeybunch can give you warm milk for that." Daddy smiled and kissed him better. "Rabbity can have some too."

"Run along now; we'll be fine," said
Mrs. Honeybunch kindly. Mommy was
looking as worried as Hopscotch.

Hopscotch and Rabbity pressed their noses to the good-bye window, still waving long after Mommy and Daddy had turned the corner out of sight.

"Now, Hopscotch," said Mrs. Honeybunch, "what shall
we do? Shall we paint a picture?"
Hopscotch and Rabbity just pressed their noses closer
to the good-bye window and gave a little sniff.

"What about building a car?"
suggested Mrs. Honeybunch.
They gave a slightly bigger sniff.

"I know!" said Mrs. Honeybunch
brightly. "Let's play hide-and-seek."
Hopscotch shook his head sadly.
"No, thank you." He sighed. "I think
I will play hiding and no seeking
all by myself."

And off he went to hide in the special No Babysitters Allowed camp that he had made earlier in the day. Rabbity stood guard outside.

Hiding is fun when someone is seeking, but hiding on your own when no one is looking for you is very boring,

as Hopscotch soon discovered.

There was not much to do in his camp, especially with
Rabbity on guard duty.

It might have been fun to build a car, or paint a picture ...

So when he heard Mrs. Honeybunch ask if Rabbity
would like to hear a story while he guarded the entrance,
Hopscotch pricked up his ears, especially because it was
one of his favorite bedtime stories.

But then the strangest thing happened. Mrs. Honeybunch got the story mixed up! She started in the middle, confused all the names, and then made up the story altogether. And she did this with not one book, not two, but *three*, until Hopscotch couldn't stand it anymore . . .

...and burst out of his camp.

"Mrs. Honeybunch," he said, "you're reading the stories
all wrong. You're mixed up."

"Oh dear, sweetheart, am I?" Mrs. Honeybunch smiled.
"Perhaps you could help me out."

So Hopscotch very patiently told Mrs. Honeybunch
about the stories in the books . . .

...and then showed her how to
build a race car, and, last of all,
how to paint a picture of a lovely
sunny day.

Then Mrs. Honeybunch
showed Hopscotch how to
make delicious warm milk
and tucked him into bed.

Much later that evening, Mommy tiptoed into his bedroom to give him a kiss good night.

"How is your tummy, sweetheart?" she asked.

"My tummy isn't worried anymore," whispered Hopscotch sleepily. "And if she wants, Mrs. Honeybunch can come and play again."